Editor Tony Tedone Publications

ISBN# 9798630775146

MiLLiE

Join Millie on her adventures to visit special friends and places.
Watch as her magical wings change colors depending on her mood,
and sometimes her food, as she shares her stories.
Come along for a visit!

Barkley, wake up.
Yaaaaawwwwwnnnn, someone is up early.

I'm going to the beach today to visit some friends. I want to see the sunrise.
Make sure to eat breakfast, and don't forget your sunscreen!

Oooooh these are
perfect for the beach;
I'll match the sun!

Who is making all that noise?!
It's just me, Wallter.
I'm stopping by to have breakfast and say hi.
Oh, well hello Millie. Just keep it down please, it's early.

NUSSBAUM INC.
Wow!
So many of my beach buddies all woke up to see the sunrise, just like me.

Hi, Everyone!
I'll be right back to play.

Hi starfish, my name is Millie.
My friends and I are going to play games, would you like to play with us?
Hello Millie, I'm Sophia.
Ummm, well I'd love to join, but I'm not like those other starfish.

See Millie, I lost an arm and I'm afraid your friends might make fun of me.
I didn't even notice Sophia. Besides, my friends are really great!

Come on everybody, let's search for sand dollars and sea glass.

Wow! What a great place to play.

HEY EVERYBODY! Come see the sandcastle.

NUSSBAUM INC.

SUN
JZ

Thank you for inviting me Millie.
This was the most fun I've ever had, and nobody even noticed my missing arm!
I'm so happy you had a great day, Sophia.

You were so busy having fun that you didn't even notice your arm is growing!
Oh my! You're right, it did grow!

It's time for me to get home. Thanks everyone for such a fun day at the beach!
Thank you, Millie, for being such a great friend.
Bye.
Bye!
Bye.
Bye!
Bye!
Bye.
Bye.
Bye.
Bye.
Bye.

What an amazing day I had! I saw some old friends and made lots of new ones.
My-my that does sound like a big day. Get some rest, tomorrow is another chance for more adventures.

It's okay to be different. It's what makes us SPECIAL!

FUN FACT!

When a starfish loses or damages an arm, the arm will grow back, as good as new.

When a Liver is split for "Live" organ donation, both halves will grow back, as good as new.

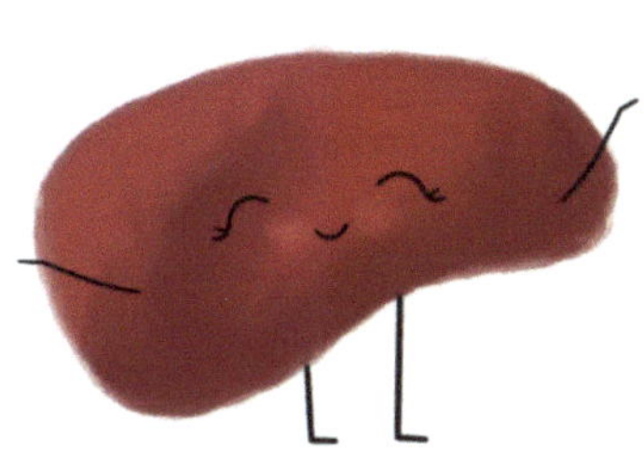

Sophia's Story

On March 16, 2017, an angel bestowed a precious gift upon Sophia that few are lucky to receive – a second chance at life. At age four, Sophia was the recipient of a liver transplant at UPMC Children's Hospital of Pittsburgh. The surgery was a symphony performed by the heroic abdominal transplant team of surgeons including Dr. Bond, Dr. Mazariegos, Dr. Soltys, Dr. Sindhi and many others.

Without a liver transplant, Sophia's quality of life and future were in question. At 18 months she was diagnosed with a rare genetic disorder when her liver stopped properly processing protein. Instead of breaking it down, protein became toxic and Sophia spent three years battling with many nights at Boston Children's Hospital. While there, she was in the greatest care possible of Dr. Berry and the many incredible ICU teams.

After 10 weeks in Pittsburgh, we eagerly returned home to the outstretched arms of family and friends to begin the journey to heal. The journey continues four years later but Sophia is thriving – a lover of children and animals, an avid reader and aspiring gymnast.

Sophia is destined for greatness, no doubt, and wouldn't be on that path without Donate Life and her angel's gift.

The McZaine's story

On June 6th, 2017 this angel on earth, as I call her, gave me a gift that can't be bought in a store, made with a 3D printer, or found on Amazon. She gave me the right lobe of her liver (Yup, the big half.) After a long recovery for the two of us, I'm happy to say that we're both doing well. Jodi's liver has grown back to full function and she has a "special" tattoo that only hero's can get. Best of all, I am the new owner of a sassy Jiver (not a typo, Jodi Liver = Jiver).   To read more about our journey, visit our transplant blog @ www.mczaines.blogspot.com

#Blessedbeyondwords #ForeverGrateful #LiveLoveLaugh

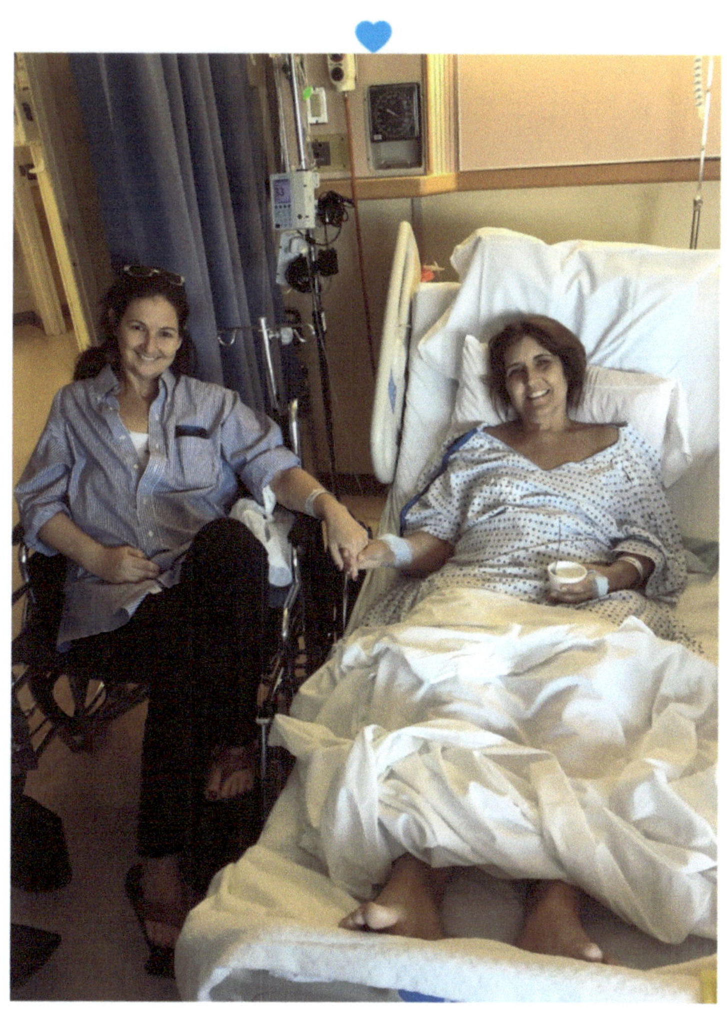

"Millie's Adventures" are not only a stories, characters or creations about learning or kindness, it's my opportunity to spread awareness about the importance of Organ Donation. Donate Life has had a personal impact on the life of not only my family, but myself. On 1/23/17 we received the news "We Matched", and so began the journey of the "Liver Divas". Visit our story @ www.mczaines.blogspot.com. Then on June 6th, 2017, Jodi courageously gave me the gift of her "Jiver"

During my recovery I was able to finish a dream I started back in 2006 "Millie's Adventures". My 1st story was a dedication to a family dear to me that suffered a tragic loss of their daughter. "Millie visits the lake" is a tribute to Melissa "Joy" Molin and her family. Now, three years later I am blessed to present "Millie visits the beach." A story about kindness and friendship, along with a clever way of sharing how amazing our bodies can heal.

A percentage of proceeds from each book sold will be donated to local Pediatric Transplant hospitals and/or Donate Life.

Becoming an organ/tissue donor is quite simple. You many either register at your local DMV upon licensing or renewal, or you may go to **ANY** of the following sites.

https://registerme.org - Fill in your information – click SUBMIT - It's that simple.

http://www.ctorganandtissuedonation.org – select "Register Me" fill in your information - SUBMIT

https://www.donatelife.net – select "Register to be a Donor", fill in your information - SUBMIT

IPhone & Android: Go to your health app on your phone & register there.

There are over 100,000 people currently on "Wait Lists". One life can save up to eight (8) lives.

"Tomorrow is not guaranteed, each day is a gift."